I0627440

Railroad Santa
and the
Holiday Train

William G. Grice, III - Author

ISBN: 978-1-965108-32-1

LCCN: 2024918385

Acknowledgements

The idea for this story developed from many people I've known and experiences I've shared with volunteers and friends who have created holiday decorations for classrooms, gymnasiums, local parks, Santa houses, church halls, Holiday Train railroad cars, and so many other places, inside and outside, along with those who have baked cookies, poured hot chocolate, handed-out candy canes, lifted their voices in holiday songs and carols, played instruments, dressed up as Elves and Santa's Helpers, and especially those who've worn the "Red Suit" to let children climb up and sit on their laps to express their hopes and wishes for the Holidays. To each and every one of you, near and far, past and present, who volunteer and bring the Holidays to life, Thank You.

Dedications

With Gratitude and Appreciation, This Book Is Dedicated to All the Volunteers who generously offer their time and talents, their treasures and creative efforts, to bring each and every Holiday celebration to life….

…to Everyone whose words and deeds share kindness and affection that provides hope and comfort to the young and the young-at-heart…,

…to my wife Ann, our four sons and daughters-in-laws: Paul & Sandy, William IV & Shannon, Jonathan & Anna, Christopher & Ashley; and to ALL of our grandchildren….

…to Family and Friends, near and far, who consistently offer their support and affection along the journeys of life we all share….

…to Railroad Workers and Rail Fans who hear the sound of a locomotive – the whistle, the bell, the clickety-clack of wheels rolling over a crossing – and feel the call for adventure….

…and to Everyone who finds pleasure in reading this book for themselves, and discovers even more pleasure in reading this story to a child.

Enter into the story of a Holiday Train.

Meet James, the Railroad Santa.

All Aboard!

William G. Grice, III

James was a railroad engineer.

Ever since he was a young boy, James loved trains and everything to do with railroads.

Eventually, as James grew-up and matured, he finished school, got a job with the railroad, and became an engineer.

1230
1230

James drove big, powerful locomotives that pulled long freight trains filled with coal and grain, chemicals, and all the important things people need, like food and clothing.

As the train moved along the tracks over mountains and across the plains, through fields and forests, James liked to wave to children and adults.

He liked to ring the bell and blow the locomotive's whistle as a way to say, "Hello" and to "Be Careful" around trains and railroad tracks.

1230
1230
1230

But there was one train James never had a
chance to drive: the Holiday Train.

Each December, the railroad had a special
train. It was called the 'Holiday Train.'

1849

The Holiday Train hauled cars for railroad officials and volunteers who dressed up as Elves and Santa's helpers.

There was a parlor car where everyone could relax.

There was a sleeper car where they could spend the night, and there was a dining car where the officials and volunteers could eat their meals.

But the most fun and exciting parts of the Holiday Train were the cars for the children to visit and see.

There was a flat car that displayed Santa's sleigh and flying reindeers.

There were four railway cars.

The first car was filled with a beautiful forest of decorated trees.

The second car showed Elves making toys and wrapping packages in the North Pole workshop.

The third car looked like a kitchen filled with holiday treats and goodies, cookies and fruits, juice and hot chocolate with marshmallows, for everyone to enjoy.

And the fourth car showed villages with small houses and buildings and toy trains running around and around and around in a circle.

Best of all, the last car on the Holiday Train was a caboose.

That's where children could wait their turn to visit with the railroad's Santa.

All along the railroad line, the Holiday Train
would stop at large cities and small towns.

At every station people would wait on the
platform, then step on board the Holiday Train
once it arrived.

1849

Everybody loved to see the Holiday Train arrive.

However, after several hours, everyone felt sad to see the Holiday Train leave and travel along the tracks to stop at the next town where more children and adults were waiting.

One day, James received a telephone call. The person calling was the Roadmaster at the depot.

"James," he said, "I just got a call from the head office. It's about the Holiday Train."

James felt excited. "Do they want me to be the engineer?" he asked hopefully.

"Well, no," the Roadmaster said. "They need someone to dress up as this year's Railroad Santa. Will you do it?"

At first, James felt sad.

He wanted to drive the locomotive and wave
out the window to all the girls and boys and
adults who came to see the Holiday Train.

Quietly, James took a minute to think about it.

Then he made a decision.

"All right," he said. "That will be fine. I'll do it.
I'll be the Railroad Santa on the Holiday
Train."

Several days later, James came to the railroad yard where the Holiday Train was being assembled. Switch engines moved railcars from one track to another to couple each one in its right place.

James knew the Holiday Train was almost ready to depart and be on its way.

1849

Along with railroad officials and volunteers,
James climbed onto the Holiday Train.

He saw the Conductor in charge of the Holiday
Train standing there looking at her watch.

She seemed impatient and very busy. She had
a lot of things on her mind.

She looked at James.

She frowned.

She didn't say "Hello."

"You must be the Santa Claus," she said. "Have
you ever been Railroad Santa before?"

James looked at the Conductor.

He shook his head. "No, mam'," he said. "I'm just an engineer. I drive locomotives that pull freight trains."

The Conductor handed James a box with the Santa suit inside. "Go to that room and put on your suit," she ordered. "Hurry up! We are about to leave."

Then she said, "Always remember to do a good job. You're working for the railroad, you know."

"Oh, yes mam'," James answered. "I'll certainly try because when I put on this suit, I'll be working for the real Santa Claus, too."

James smiled, but the Conductor in charge
just walked away.

Santa
Suit

Soon the Holiday Train started to move. It moved along the tracks.

After traveling many miles, it stopped at a station where girls and boys, parents and grandparents, aunts and uncles, neighbors and friends were waiting on the platform.

Volunteer helpers, and some were dressed up like Elves, handed out candy canes.

A band of singers sang songs and musicians played instruments. Everyone was eager to climb on board the Holiday Train to see the beautiful decorations in each of the rail cars.

HoLIDAY
TRAIN

All the children were excited to see Railroad Santa in the caboose to tell him what gifts they'd like to receive during the holidays.

Dressed as Santa Claus, James sat in a large chair. He saw many children who had waited in line.

 Some children placed their notes and letters inside Railroad Santa's Mail Box. Each note and letter expressed a special greeting or wish, and, of course, what they would like for holiday gifts.

That evening, just before the Holiday Train
was about to leave, a girl who stood at the end
of the line finally had her turn to visit Railroad
Santa.

She had waited a long time.

The girl climbed up on Santa's lap. She
whispered in his ear.

Then, the girl began to cry.

Santa looked sad and concerned.

He thought for a moment.

Then, Santa whispered some words into the girl's ear.

The girl smiled. She nodded her head.

She gave Santa a hug, climbed off his lap, and walked out of the caboose with her parents.

The Conductor in charge of the Holiday Train was watching James.

When the girl left the caboose, the Conductor walked over to Santa.

"James," she demanded, "what did you say to make that little girl cry?"

James looked surprised.

He said, "Why, nothing at all."

"Well, then," said the Conductor, "what did she say to you?"

"That girl climbed on my lap and told me what she wanted for the Holidays," James said. "She told me her grandparent was sick and that her parents were very worried. The only gift she wanted was for her grandparent to get better."

The Conductor in charged looked stunned. "What did you say to her?" she wanted to know.

"Before I tell you," said James, "let me ask you a question. What would you say to a girl or boy who wants a family member or friend to get better?"

The Conductor in charge became very quiet.

She looked puzzled.

Then, she shook her head. "That's a hard question to answer," she said. "I don't know what I would say."

"Well," said James, "I told that little girl, 'In your heart you know that Santa can't always give children what they want, but I also want you to know in your heart that Santa loves you and Santa will always try.'"

With tears of joy in her eyes, the Conductor in charge of the Holiday Train smiled.

James smiled, too.

"You did well, James," she said. And the Conductor gave him a hug. "You're the very best Railroad Santa this railroad has ever had."

James smiled. "Thank you," he said. "All I wanted to do was to be kind, honest, and caring. And, of course, I wanted to try to be just like Santa."

The End